HIEROGLYPHS
The Writing of Ancient Egypt

The hieroglyph on the opposite page, which means "writing," shows the scribe's equipment: his palette, bag for the pigment, and reed holder.

HIEROGLYPHS
The Writing of Ancient Egypt

NORMA JEAN KATAN

WITH BARBARA MINTZ

Margaret K. McElderry Books

Margaret K. McElderry Books
An imprint of Simon & Schuster Children's Publishing Division
1230 Avenue of the Americas
New York, New York 10020

Designed by Maria Epes

11   13   15   17   19   20   18   16   14   12

LIBRARY OF CONGRESS CATALOGING IN PUBLICATION DATA

Katan, Norma Jean.
  Hieroglyphs, the writing of ancient Egypt.

  "A Margaret K. McElderry book."
  SUMMARY: Introduces hieroglyphs commonly found on tombs, statues, funerary objects, and amulets, explains their origins, and presents instructions for drawing them.
    1. Egyptian language—Writing, Hieroglyphic—Juvenile literature. 1. Egyptian language—Writing, Hieroglyphic. 2. Hieroglyphs
  I. Mintz, Barbara. II. Title.
  PJ1097.K3   493'.1   80-13576
  ISBN 0-689-50176-5

ACKNOWLEDGMENTS

I would like to thank Vicki Solia, Researcher in the Department of Egyptian and Classical Art at The Brooklyn Museum, for all her help in securing the illustrations and Diane Guzman, Librarian of the Wilbour Library of Egyptology at The Brooklyn Museum, for providing help in the research of this book; and I especially wish to thank Paula Schwartz for her invaluable assistance, counsel, and direction throughout the writing of this book.　　　　　NJK

The Rosetta Stone
Basalt
196 B.C.
The British Museum

HIEROGLYPHS are the signs or letters of ancient Egyptian writing. Each sign is a picture of something that was familiar to the ancient Egyptians, such as an old man leaning on a stick, a cow suckling her calf, a clump of papyrus, or a boat. There are over seven hundred of these signs. This book will show you some of these hieroglyphs and give some of the rules for reading and writing them. You will be able to recognize many of the signs when you see them in Egyptian paintings and carved on Egyptian tombs and sculpture.

In ancient times, as it is today, Egypt was divided into Upper and Lower Egypt. It may seem confusing to us when we look at the map to see Upper Egypt at the bottom, or the south, and Lower Egypt at the top, or the north. The reason for this is that the Nile River flows from south to north. Therefore upstream, or south, means Upper Egypt, and down-downstream, or north, means Lower Egypt.

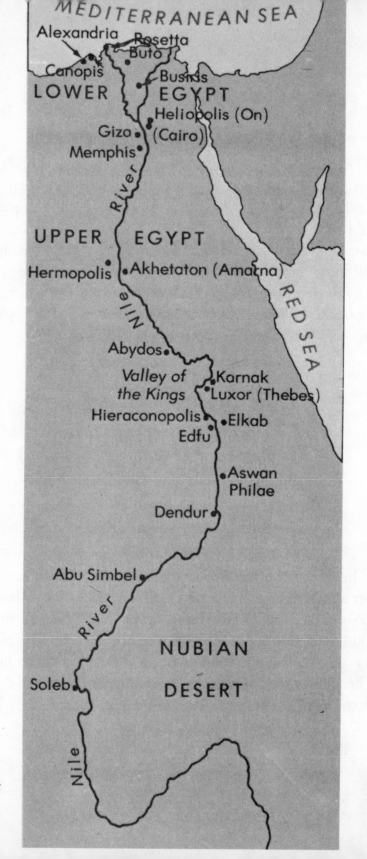

In Upper Egypt, along the banks of the Nile, there was only a narrow strip of fertile land, often less than a hundred yards wide, on which people could farm. The rest was desert. But in Lower Egypt, there was more land that was usable for farming — in some places the strip was more than a hundred miles wide.

The river served as an important travel route. Most of the great temples and pyramids of Egypt were built along the Nile or near it. Building materials were transported by barge on the Nile, and visitors could easily reach the temples by river. Most of the inscriptions on tombs and wall fragments that you see in museums come from temples and tombs near the Nile.

At one time Upper and Lower Egypt were two different lands, each ruled by a different king and each king wearing a different crown. The king of Upper Egypt wore a white crown. The king of Lower Egypt wore a red crown. The two kingdoms were united under King Narmer in 3100 B.C., and after that the sign of the ruler of both lands was a double crown.

White Crown   *Red Crown*   *Double Crown*

Egyptian history is divided into large periods of time called kingdoms: the Old Kingdom, the Middle Kingdom and the New Kingdom. Each one of these periods is divided into dynasties. Each dynasty is a period of time during which rulers of one family governed Egypt. It is useful to know when these periods were, because that is how most scholars have dated the paintings and sculptures you see in museums. At the end of the book you will find a list of kingdoms, dynasties, and the names of the most important Egyptian kings.

Hieroglyphs were carved and painted on the walls of tombs, temples, and pyramids, as well as on statues. They were even used on everyday things, such as mirrors, furniture, and games. Hieroglyphs not only added to the beauty of these objects; they had another purpose — a magical one.

Ancient Egyptians believed in a life after death, a life that they hoped would be like their life on earth, only better. They believed that words had magical powers and that if they wrote the name of a thing they needed and put the writing in their tomb they would be sure to have that thing in the next life.

Early in his or her lifetime every Egyptian who could afford to planned and built his or her tomb with the help of an architect and masons, scribes, and artisans. It was furnished with things the person would need for a comfortable afterlife, such as food, chairs, beds, clothing, jewelry, and games. Because the ancient Egyptians believed so strongly in the power of the written words, the names of these things were not only written on the objects themselves, they were also painted or carved on the tomb walls, so that in case robbers stole the dead person's possessions they would still "be" there.

Ancient Egyptians called their writing "words of the gods" because they believed that Thoth, the god of learning, had invented writing. The word *hieroglyph* was first used to name these signs in 300 B.C., when the Greeks came to Egypt and saw them carved on the temple walls. In Greek, *hiero* means "holy" and *glyph* means "writing."

Ceremonial mirror with gods incised on it
Bronze (disk) and wood (handle)
Dynasty 26, around 600 B.C.
The Brooklyn Museum

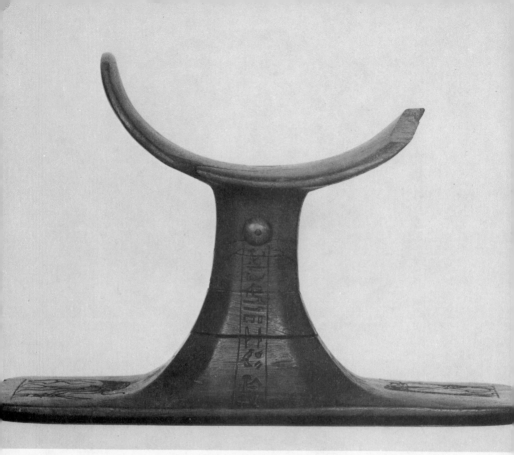

Headrest inscribed for the owner, Yuwy
Wood
Dynasty 18, around 1470 B.C.
The Brooklyn Museum

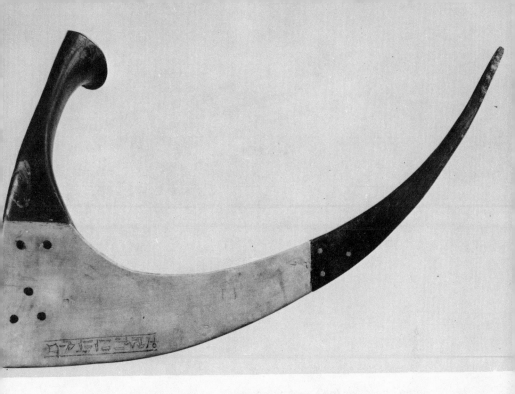

Sickle used for harvesting grain in the afterlife and belonging to a
farmer, Amenemhat, at Thebes. Amenemhat was a common name in
ancient Egypt and appeared frequently in inscriptions.

Wood and ivory
Dynasty 18, around 1460 B.C.
The Brooklyn Museum

Gameboard for the Senet game
Wood, ivory, and faience
Dynasty 18, around 1450 B.C.
Metropolitan Museum of Art

14

Shawabty (figurine of a farm laborer for the afterlife) of Amenemhat,
   a scribe, holding hoes and seed bags
Wood
Dynasty 18, around 1480 B.C.
The Brooklyn Museum

After the Greeks, led by Alexander the Great, conquered Egypt in the fourth century B.C., the ancient Egyptian language was gradually forgotten and Greek was spoken and written all over Egypt. Finally only a few priests were left who could write hieroglyphs.

For almost two thousand years after that hieroglyphic writing was a mystery no one could solve, though many people tried to. Then in 1799 Napoleon led an expedition to Egypt. There, in a place called Rosetta, his soldiers found a slab of stone that did not look like anything else they had seen in Egypt. It was about four feet high, and it was covered with what seemed to be three completely different kinds of writing. One of the texts was written in Egyptian hieroglyphs. Napoleon and everyone else who saw the stone began to suspect that these texts said the same thing in three different languages. If this was true, and one of the languages could be read, it would mean that they had finally found a way to decipher Egyptian hieroglyphs.

Scholars soon found that the second of the three texts was written in *demotic*, a shorthand script that developed around 700 B.C. from *hieratic*. Hieratic is a cursive version of hieroglyphic writing. The third text was written in Greek. The stone on which these three texts were carved became known all over the world as the Rosetta Stone.

The man who eventually solved the mystery was a young Frenchman named Jean François Champollion. He had always been fascinated by languages. When he was eleven someone showed him some hieroglyphs and told him that no one in the world could read them. Right then he made up his mind to be the one to decipher them. He learned eleven languages, including Greek and Hebrew, and he studied the Rosetta Stone

Detail of the cartouches of Ptolemy on the Rosetta Stone
Basalt
196 B.C.
The British Museum
(See also photograph facing first page of text.)

for twenty years. He noticed that certain signs in the Egyptian hieroglyphic text were enclosed like this in an oval called a *cartouche*.

Champollion suspected that these words were the names of rulers, and that the oval ring around them was to show that they were especially important. Knowing that the names of

P   T   O   L

C   L   I   O   P   A

two rulers, Cleopatra and Ptolemy, appeared frequently in the Greek text, he thought that the signs enclosed within oval rings in the Egyptian text might stand for these same rulers. Up until then scholars had believed that each sign represented a picture. Instead, Champollion matched the signs within the ovals in the hieroglyphic text with the name of Ptolemy. In doing so, he connected each of the signs with a sound instead of a picture and was able to recognize the name of Ptolemy on the Rosetta Stone and that of Cleopatra on another ancient monument because her cartouche, the oval containing her name, is broken off the top of the hieroglyphic section of the Rosetta Stone.

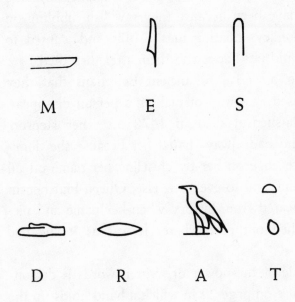

M   E   S

D   R   A   T

(Feminine names end in "t.")

The egg (o) indicates that it is the name of a woman. (It is not pronounced.)

This was the breakthrough that he needed to decipher the rest of the text. The year was 1822.

Written words in ancient Egypt had great power for the afterlife. They were not just symbols for real things and ideas; they almost *were* the things they needed. In some tombs, hieroglyphs that represented evil animals were drawn without legs or heads, or chopped in half, or even nailed down so that the "animals" could not eat the food that was left in the tomb for the dead person to eat in the next life. The hieroglyph of a snake was sometimes left whole, though, because it would not be interested in eating human food.

The hieroglyph of the fish was hardly ever shown on a tomb wall, because ancient Egyptians thought fish might harm the dead. This may have been because they saw fish nibbling on dead dogs and donkeys floating in the Nile and wanted to make sure this would not happen to them after they died.

Words were so powerful to ancient Egyptians that they were sometimes used as a way of making a person disappear. When Queen Hatshepsut died in 1470 B.C., her stepson, Tuthmosis III, who had always hated her because she dominated him, took revenge on her by chiseling her name off all her temples. To him, and to everyone else, Queen Hatshepsut completely disappeared from history when her name and pictures were scratched out everywhere. It was as if she had never existed.

Another example of the power of written words is demonstrated in the picture on page 22 in which a hand holds up the hieroglyph for "life," which the ancient Egyptians called *ankh*, to the nose of Queen Nefertiti, the wife of King Akhenaten, who ruled in Dynasty 18, 1360 B.C.

Evil animal (snake) pinned down by knives (in upper left corner)
Wood
Dynasty 18, around 1370 B.C.
Thebes, Tomb of Kheru-ef

Ankh sign held to the nose of Queen Nefertiti
Sandstone
Dynasty 18, around 1360 B.C.
The Brooklyn Museum

Erased figure of Queen Hatshepsut between two gods, Horus on left and Thoth on right

Dynasty 18, around 1480 B.C.
Karnak, Temple of Amun

Ancient Egyptians believed that the nose was the "seat of life." To destroy an enemy forever was a simple matter. It could be done by smashing the nose of a statue or on any other representation of the person. To hold the *ankh* sign to Queen Nefertiti's nose magically guaranteed her eternal life.

Words with magic power were also carved or painted on a stela, a slab of stone. Sometimes a stela is horizontal, as in the stela of Ma'ety, a gatekeeper, smelling a jar of sweet oil on page 29.

Sometimes a stela is vertical. And sometimes the upper part is carved in a semicircle like the one on page 28.

Stelae were used for many purposes. They were placed either against a wall or built into one. Since the ancient Egyptians believed they needed food for their afterlife, they made a written contract during their lifetime with priests and relatives. The priests and relatives agreed to bring the food to the tomb after the person had died and place it on an offering table that looked like the one on page 28.

Wepem-nofret was a high official during the 4th Dynasty, around 2600 B.C. In this stela, facing Wepem-nofret, are hieroglyphs of things he needed for his afterlife. This is called an offering list. The pictures of food in Wepem-nofret's offering list were not just pictures. They were signs that could magically become real food in the next life if, by chance, real food were not left on the offering table. The name and profession of the dead person, as well as his or her picture, were always shown on the offering list.

Here is another offering list from Dynasty 5, later than Wepem-nofret's. After Dynasty 5 it became a standard formula:

Painted stela of Wepem-nofret
Limestone
Dynasty 4, around 2600 B.C.
Berkeley, Lowie Museum of Anthropology

1000 jugs of wine

1000 loaves of bread

1000 cattle

1000 geese

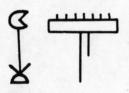

1000 alabaster jars

1000 pieces of cloth

All things good and clean

Stela of Sen-res and his wife holding a lotus, at an offering table
Limestone
Dynasty 18, around 1480 B.C.
The Brooklyn Museum

Stela of Ma'ety, a gatekeeper, smelling a jar of sweet oil
Limestone
Dynasty 11, around 2040 B.C.
Metropolitan Museum of Art

Worshiping scene on a stela
Basalt
Dynasty 25, around 700 B.C.
The Brooklyn Museum

Stela of a sculptor named Imeny
Limestone
Dynasty 12, around 1900 B.C.
Paris, Louvre

Stela of Nefer-iu in form of a false door
Limestone
Dynasty 10, around 2100
Metropolitan Museum of Art

Page 32 shows a stela of Nefer-iu. It is called a *false door stela*, because the inner part is shaped like the opening of a door. It was placed on a wall within the tomb so that a dead person could return from the afterlife through the "door" and find the "food" that his or her relatives or the priests had left. The dead person could then leave through the "door."

On page 36 is a painting of a hunt. The name of the hunter is Nakht. He was a scribe of the granaries during the 18th Dynasty. Nakht had this bird-hunting scene painted to make sure that the pleasure of this sport would magically continue for him in his next life after death. His name was written in hieroglyphs on the painting like this:

Like all ancient Egyptians, Nakht believed that if his name was written it — and he — would exist after his death. Prayers and hymns to the gods were spoken and sung at kings' or queens' funerals to help them on their journey through the underworld, through which they must pass on their way to heaven. We call these prayers for dead rulers of the Old Kingdom, *Pyramid Texts*, because they were written on the walls of burial chambers in pyramids.

The Pyramid Texts assured any ruler who used them of a safe place in the afterworld. With the help of these writings he or she would be able to defeat all monsters and demons that they might meet on their way to heaven.

Coffin Texts, painted on the coffin of a nobleman, Gua
Early Dynasty 12, around 2000 B.C.
The British Museum

Another version of these prayers was used during the Middle Kingdom. Because they were written on the inside of wooden coffins and on coffin lids, these inscriptions are called *Coffin Texts*. The Pyramid Texts could only be used by kings and queens, but the Coffin Texts could be used by noblemen and other important people. They gave protection against hunger, thirst, and the dangers of the underworld. They also gave the dead person the power to change into whatever form he or she wanted to take in the next life and guaranteed that the life would be a happy one.

In the New Kingdom there was a third version of these magical texts, which was for sale only to well-to-do Egyptians as it was expensive. It is believed that priests sold them at temples. We call them *Books of the Dead*, though they are not in books. They are a collection of religious sayings and magical texts that were read and chanted during funerals. These prayers and spells were written on papyrus or leather and often put into a wooden box decorated with a statuette of the god Osiris-Sokaris and placed within the linen wrappings of the mummy. Their purpose was to guarantee a happy afterlife for the dead person.

There are 190 "chapters" (or sections) of The Book of the Dead, but as far as we know, no one bought the entire manuscript. Each person chose those chapters that he or she particularly wanted or could afford to have copied. Members of royal families, priests, or scribes sometimes bought expensive copies and had them illustrated by well-known artists.

Other copies were prepared with blank spaces left, so that the name of the person who bought one could be added later. Also, during the 18th Dynasty texts from The Book of the Dead were painted on the walls of the tombs of noblemen.

Painting of Nakht, a nobleman, hunting in the marshes
Dynasty 18, around 1400 B.C.
Thebes, Tomb of Nakht

Relief of Hagy being presented by his son with a goose
Limestone
Dynasty 7–8, around 2170 B.C.
Paris, Louvre

Sometimes four bricks inscribed with short texts from The Book of the Dead were placed in niches in the four walls of the tomb chamber, to keep the dead person's enemies from attacking the body. These enemies could come from the north, south, east, or west, and so four bricks were needed to keep them away.

The people who knew how to read and write hieroglyphs were called *scribes*. Since few Egyptians knew how to read and write, those who did were highly respected. It was the greatest ambition of many parents to have their children educated to become scribes.

We know that some girls were taught to read and write, because writing tools were found in the tomb of two of King Akhenaten's daughters. It is unlikely, however, that girls from less important families were taught to read and write.

As a rule, a boy in ancient Egypt entered the same profession as his father: a baker's son became a baker and a sandalmaker's son became a sandalmaker. Only by learning how to read and write hieroglyphs could a boy break from the family tradition, and by becoming a scribe, he was able to enter the higher ranks of society.

The schooling of a scribe began at an early age and was completed at sixteen. To become a scribe meant ten to twelve years of hard training. The first step for some was to enter a special school at a royal palace. There the boy was taught with the children of the royal family. Children from noble but not necessarily rich families were sent to schools attached to temples, where they were taught by priests. Children from poor families, if they were talented, were taught by the village scribe, who usually taught his own children and those of his relatives.

Scribe school was a long and difficult course of study. At first the young apprentice had to memorize the signs or letters of the hieroglyphic alphabet. He used pieces of pottery or limestone, called *ostraka*, and wooden boards that were covered with a white coating called *gesso*, a mixture of plaster and glue, on which to practice writing "letters," or signs, with a brush.

When a student became more skilled at writing hieroglyphs, he was allowed to use papyrus, which is a paperlike material made from the stem of the papyrus plant. Beginners could not use papyrus because it was too expensive.

The scribe's writing tools consisted of a palette that held two cakes of ink, one red and one black; a pot of water to moisten the ink; brushes of various sizes; and a brush holder. He made his brushes by cutting the tip of a papyrus reed at an angle and sucking it to make it soft. These tools were light and easy for the scribe to carry with him, as you can see in the photographs on pages 40 and 41.

The young scribe not only learned to write hieroglyphs, but he also learned to write *hieratic*, which was the form of cursive writing. In writing hieratic script, the hieroglyphs were connected as in our handwriting. It differs from hieroglyphs in the same way that our script handwriting differs from our printing. Hieratic was used mainly for everyday business matters.

By copying and recopying many different types of letters and texts, the young scribe became educated in literature, religion, mathematics, and medicine. Scribe school was not easy, as we learn from an inscription on an ancient papyrus: *"Spend no day in idleness or thou wilt be beaten."* However, it must have seemed worth the effort.

On another ancient papyrus, a father tells a son how much

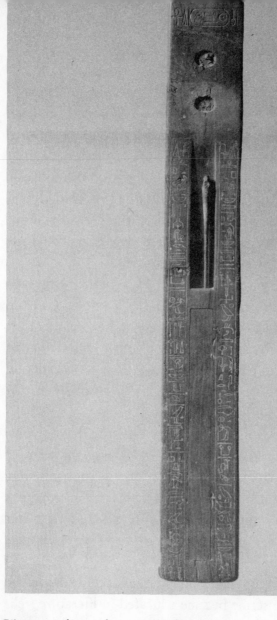

Writing palette of a man called Neb-iry
Wood
Dynasty 18, around 1450 B.C.
Berkeley, Lowie Museum of Anthropology

Tools of a scribe: reed holder, container of color, and mixing palette
Late Period, around 700 B.C.
Chicago, Oriental Institute Museum

Sculptor's trial piece showing exercise for carving hieroglyphs
Limestone
Around 1000 B.C.
The Brooklyn Museum

hieroglyphs

hieroglyphs

Examples of script and block letters

Example of hieratic writing: The Great Harris Papyrus
Dynasty 20, around 1150 B.C.
The British Museum

better it is to be a scribe than anything else:

"It is greater than any other profession. There is nothing like it on earth.

"I have seen a coppersmith at work at his furnace. His fingers were like the claws of the crocodile and he stank more than a fish.

"The jeweler . . . when he has completed the inlay work of amulets, his strength vanishes and he is tired out.

"The barber shaves until the end of the evening. But he must be up early . . . He takes himself from street to street to seek someone to shave. He wears out his arms to fill his belly.

"The potter is covered with dirt. His clothes . . . stiff with mud, his headdress . . . of rags.

"I shall describe to you the bricklayer. His kidneys hurt him.

"The weaver inside the weaving house is . . . wretched . . . He cannot breathe the air. If he wastes a single day without weaving he is beaten with fifty whip lashes . . . He has to give food to the doorkeeper to allow him to come to the daylight.

"The arrow maker is completely wretched.

"The furnace maker, his fingers are burnt . . . his eyes are inflamed because of the heaviness of the smoke.

"The washerman launders at the riverbank near the crocodiles."

After all this, the father tells the son: *"See, I have placed you on the path of God."* Clearly, he felt that being a scribe was a very good thing for his son.

After a boy's education as a scribe had been completed, he could become an accountant, a doctor, a priest, a granary foreman, a cattle foreman, a foreman of weavers, a foreman of craftsmen, a foreman of sculptors, or a private secretary to the king or a nobleman.

Here is a quotation from the Papyrus of Anastasi which shows how important and privileged scribes were in Egypt: *". . . the scribe directs every work in the land . . . for him there are no taxes . . . he payeth tribute in writing."*

Hieroglyphs show pictures of an animal or a human being or some object that was familiar to most people in ancient Egypt.

lotus   gameboard   quail chick

child   boat   owl

Hieroglyph showing a vulture and
  representing the sound "a"
Dynasty 18, around 1536 B.C.
Karnak

Hieroglyphs
Dynasty 18, around 1536 B.C.
Karnak

Hieroglyph showing an owl and
representing the sound "m"
Dynasty 18, around 1536 B.C.

In the very beginning, around five thousand years ago when hieroglyphs first appeared, these pictures meant what they showed. A picture of a mat meant a mat.

☐

At about the same time, in 3100 B.C., when King Narmer became the first king of Upper and Lower Egypt, some of these pictures or signs came to stand for the sound that the original Egyptian word began with. The sign for mat no longer stood for a mat, as it had before, but now stood for the sound "P," because the word for mat in Egyptian is "Pe." For instance, this hieroglyph shows an owl, and it stands for the letter M, with which the Egyptian word for owl began, and it sounds like our "M" in mother. Following are the twenty-four signs of the hieroglyphic alphabet, called phonograms. Each hieroglyph is followed by the name of what it represents and by the sound for which it stands.

a vulture   A as in AH

a reed leaf   I as in SIT

two reed leaves   has two sounds:
                     EE as in SEE
                     Y as in YES

an arm and
a hand   A as in BARK

a baby quail   has two sounds:
                     W as in WON
                     OO as in MOVE

a foot   B as in BAT

□ a mat   P as in PUPPY

 a horned snake   F as in FAT

an owl   M as in MUMMY

water   N as in NO

 mouth   R as in RAT

courtyard   H as in HUT

twisted flax   H as in HA

placenta   CH as in LOCH Ness Monster

 animal belly with teats   CK as in LOCK

folded cloth

 a door bolt   S as in SIT

a pool   SH as in SHOE

a hillside   QU as in QUICK

a basket with   K as in KITTEN
handle

a stool   G as in GOLD

a loaf of bread   T as in TART

54

a rope   CH as in CHAIR

a hand   D as in DIRT

 a snake   DJ as in EDGE

There are other phonograms or sound signs that stand not for one but two letters: they are a combination of two consonants and made complete words in the ancient Egyptian language. The ancient Egyptians didn't write most vowels. As we read them, we usually provide a short "e," as in "met," between consonants.

is n + b and is pronounced *neb*. It means "everyone" and "lord."

is p + r and is pronounced *per*. It means "house."

is d + w and is pronounced *jew*. It means "mountain."

There are other two-consonant phonograms.

is m + n and is pronounced *men*. It means "established" and "remain."

is m + s and is pronounced *mes*. It means "born."

There are also phonograms or sound signs that stand for *three* consonants and make complete words. For example:

is h + t + p and is pronounced *hetep*. It means "offering."

is w + s + r and is pronounced *weser*. It means "powerful."

is n + f + r and is pronounced *nefer*. It means "beautiful."

There are also many other three-consonant phonograms.

The second group of hieroglyphs are called *ideograms*. Ideograms are signs that mean what they show. Each ideogram stands for a word. They also have sounds so they can be pronounced.

is s + t and is pronounced *set*. It shows a chair and it means "chair."

is n + w + t, is pronounced *newet*. It shows the crossroads in the center of town and means "town."

Some phonograms become ideograms when a vertical stroke is drawn under the sign. For example:

As a phonogram, this sign, which shows a mouth, has the sound of R as in "rat."

When a stroke is placed underneath like this, it means "mouth."

The third group of hieroglyphs is called *determinatives*. Determinatives have no sound. They cannot be pronounced. They are used with hieroglyphs that have more than one meaning in order to make their meaning clear.

Since scribes did not write vowels, many words in Egyptian have more than one meaning. In English C + T could be read *cat* or *cot* and S + N could be read *sun* or *son*. By adding a picture at the end, the meaning of the word becomes clear to the reader.

C T 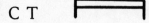   S N

C T    S N

In a similar way, many words written in hieroglyphs have more than one meaning.

can mean LOVE and MILK JAR

The first sign shows the hoe, is written MR, and is pronounced *mer*. The second sign shows the mouth, stands for the letter "R" and has the sound of *R*.

By adding the determinative of the "man with his hand to his mouth" to the word, it means LOVE.

By adding the determinative of the "jar" to the word, it becomes MILK JAR.

The determinative showing "a man sinking to the ground from fatigue" is usually used after the word meaning "tired." For example, a tired man is written like this in hieroglyphs:

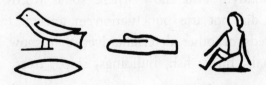

The word is composed of:

This sign shows the WR bird and is pronounced *wer*.

This sign shows the mouth and is pronounced *re*.

And this is the sign for hand and has the sound of *de*.

The word is pronounced *wered* and it means "to be tired." The determinative of "the man sinking to the ground from fatigue" is added to the signs to emphasize the meaning "to be tired."

Determinatives also show where some words end, since Egyptians did not use punctuation in ancient times. There are hundreds of other determinatives that show human beings, animals, birds, fish, buildings, ships, trees, and plants.

Here are some that have to do with sky, earth, and water:

means SKY

means NIGHT

means RAIN

These determinatives have to do with nature:

shows TREE

means PLANT or FLOWER

means VINE or GARDEN

means WOOD or TREE

means AIR, WIND or SAIL

means STAR

 means SUN or LIGHT

 means SUNSHINE

Here are determinatives that show people:

 a man striking an enemy with a stick

a seated woman

a man dancing

a man holding something on his head

a woman sitting on a chair and holding a child

a child

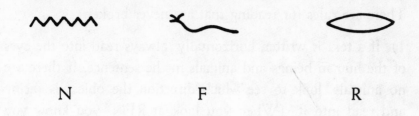

N   F   R

You have just read "nefer" from left to right, but normally the ancient Egyptian wrote from right to left or from top to bottom.

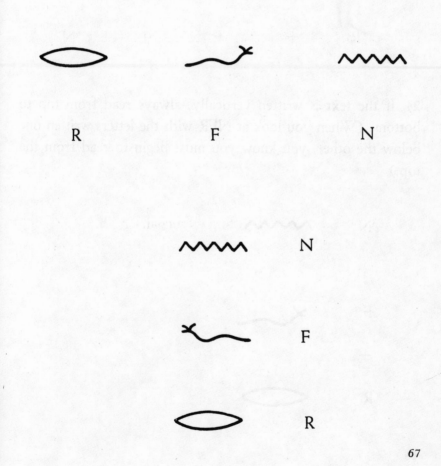

R   F   N

N

F

R

There are rules for reading that are never broken:

1) If a text is written horizontally, always read into the eyes of the human beings and animals in the sentence. If there are no animals, look to see which direction the object is facing and read into it. (When you look at RFN, you know you must read it from right to left, because the snake is facing right and you must look into its eyes.)

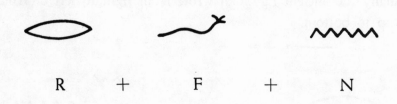

R   +   F   +   N

2) If the text is written vertically, always read from top to bottom. (When you look at NFR with the letters written one below the other, you know you must begin to read from the top.)

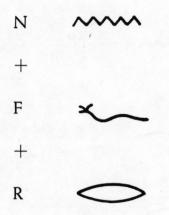

There are other rules for drawing hieroglyphs. Some hieroglyphs are always drawn to fit into an invisible square.

Some hieroglyphs fit into a half-square (vertical) or a half-
square (horizontal).

Before starting to write hieroglyphs practice these drawing
exercises until you are satisfied.

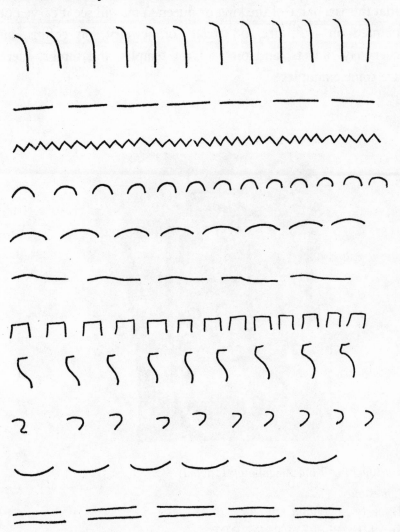

Now that you have learned the alphabet and some of the rules for reading Egyptian, you are ready to write your name, as the ancient Egyptian kings and queens did, in a cartouche (the oval ring that surrounds a royal name). You can write it vertically or horizontally and from left to right or from right to left. Whenever you see a cartouche, you will know that this is a name of the king or queen. You will see it carved or painted on sculpture, on stelae, on jewelry, on coffins, on everyday objects, and on walls of temples and tombs. Here are some examples:

Cartouche of King Amenhotep I (detail)
Limestone
Dynasty 18, around 1540 B.C.
Staatliche Museen zu Berlin/DDR

70

The side of a statue of King Sesostris I with his royal and personal
  names incised on the throne
Basalt
Dynasty 12, around 1950 B.C.
Metropolitan Museum of Art

Statue of Amenemhat, Mayor of Thebes, reading a papyrus scroll
Limestone
Dynasty 18, around 1450 B.C.
The Brooklyn Museum

There are certain groups of hieroglyphs that you will see over and over again.

is "a boon which the king gives" written in hieroglyphs.

It is composed of:

is written NSW, stands for the sedge plant, and is pronounced *nesew*.

is written HTP, stands for an offering, and is pronounced *hetep*.

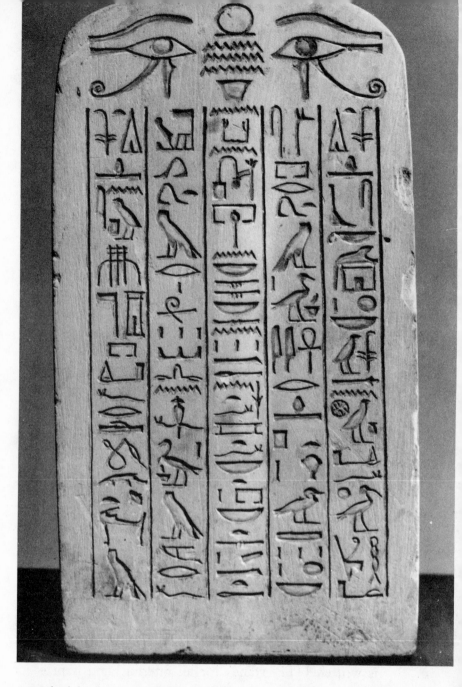

Back slab of a statue showing the offering formula twice
Limestone
Dynasty 18, around 1400 B.C.
The Brooklyn Museum

is written D, stands for a cone-shaped loaf of bread, and is pronounced *dee*.

Together, it is pronounced *hetep dee nesew*. It is written in a slightly different order than it reads.

A boon is a gift. "A boon which the king gives" is the beginning of a prayer that the ancient Egyptians wrote on their tombs, on their coffins, on their stelae. It explains that the god has received offerings from the king and that he will provide the king with everything the king needs for his life after death. You will see it often.

(also appears written)

You will also see these hieroglyphs often:

means "given life" and is pronounced *dee ankh*

is the sign for bread, as you may remember (bread is a familiar offering), and is pronounced *dee*

is the sign for life and is pronounced *ankh*

They were written after the person's name on the tomb wall and were meant to guarantee that the dead person would live forever in the next world.

 means "King of Upper
and Lower Egypt"
and is pronounced *nesew bity*.

It is composed of:

which, as you know, represents the sedge plant that
grew in Upper Egypt, and is pronounced *nesew*.

represents the sign for the letter "T" and has the
sound of *J*.

represents a bee. It was used as a sign for Lower
Egypt, perhaps because there were so many bees
there.

77

Hieroglyphs
Dynasty 18, around 1536 B.C.
Karnak

Relief of King Mentuhotep III with a goddess
Limestone
Dynasty 11, around 2000 B.C.
The Brooklyn Museum

Kings used certain signs to show that they were rulers of Upper and Lower Egypt, as shown in the relief of King Mentuhotep III on page 79.

Means "life, prosperity, and health" and is pronounced *ankh, wedja, seneb*.

shows a tie with a loop, means "life," and is pronounced *ankh*.

shows a bow-shaped drill for making fire by friction. It means "prosperity," and is pronounced *wedja*.

$\bigcap$

shows a bolt of cloth, means "healthy," and is pronounced *seneb*.

The ancient Egyptians used this on the walls of their tombs to make sure they would have life, prosperity, and health for eternity. You can write this after you sign your name on a letter, as a way of wishing your friends *ankh*, *wedja*, and *seneb* . . . life, prosperity, and health.

The ancient Egyptians also had a special system of writing numbers.

| 1 is shown by drawing a stroke

$\bigcap$ 10 is shown by drawing a cord

$\wp$ 100 is shown by drawing a coil of rope

$\c{X}$ 1000 is shown by drawing a lotus plant

10,000 is shown by drawing a finger

100,000 is shown by drawing a tadpole (the ancient Egyptian probably chose the tadpole to show 100,-000 because there are always so many of them swimming together.)

1,000,000 is shown by drawing the figure of a god with his arms raised over his head.

There are rules for reading and writing numbers in hieroglyphs:

1) The higher number is always written in front of the lower number.
2) When there is more than one row of numbers, start at the top and read down.

All numbers were written by using combinations of these

figures. For instance, 125 is written in Egyptian numbers:

32 is written:

2,200 is written:

111,000 is written:

1,000,001 is written:

*Offering list of Juthmosis III showing on top names of items
and their numbers on certain holidays*
Sandstone
Dynasty 18, around 1450 B.C.
Karnak, Jemple of Amun

You can see many of these numbers on page 84, which shows an offering list of King Tuthmosis III.

Some hieroglyphs were used as good luck charms called amulets. The ancient Egyptians wore them as jewelry and tied these charms to their wrists, neck, ankles, or waist, because they believed that the amulets had magical powers and would protect them from dangerous creatures such as crocodiles, snakes, or scorpions, and from disasters such as storms, floods, accidents, disease, or hunger.

Amulets were made of wood, gold, bronze, and various semiprecious stones such as carnelian, turquoise, and lapis lazuli. But the material most often used was faience, which was crushed quartz sand fired to look like blue or green glazed stone. Amulets were worn not only by the living but were also placed inside the linen wrappings of the dead to help them on their voyage to the next life. These amulets used with the dead were often made of less sturdy materials, cheap substitutes for hard stone, such as thin layers of metal foil or plaster, as they did not have to suffer the wear and tear of everyday life. Here are some of the amulets that were most commonly worn:

The UDJAT ("Eye of Horus") hieroglyph shows the eye of the falcon-headed god Horus. It is a combination of the human eye and the markings of a falcon's eye, which showed the black feathers under the eye. It was used as an amulet against injury. According to a myth, the eye of the god Horus was ripped out of his head by a wicked storm god called Seth. Later it was miraculously restored to Horus by the god Thoth.

Udjat eye inlaid in glass
First century B.C.
Corning Museum of Glass

The hieroglyph DJED represents a column of trimmed papyrus stalks tied together, but later the Egyptians identified it with the backbone of a god, Osiris. It is the sign for stability and was used by kings and queens to ensure a long and peaceful reign.

The SA sign represents a life preserver made out of papyrus. It was worn by the herdsman who was driving his animals through the swamp and protected him in case he fell into the water. As an amulet the SA sign was worn as a general protection against unfriendly forces.

The MES sign was used to protect women during childbirth. It represents three foxes' skins tied together. MES means "birth" in Egyptian, but no one knows why the Egyptians chose three foxes' skins for this sign.

The FISH sign provided magical powers for healing and protection against sickness. Sometimes it was worn by young girls on the end of their pigtails. It was also the good luck charm of boatmen.

The ANKH sign, as described before, represents a tie with a loop. It means "life" and therefore has more power than any other hieroglyph.

Djed pillar
Faience
Dynasty 26, around 600 B.C.
The Brooklyn Museum

Amulets are one of the most personal forms of Egyptian writing and remind us how human and like us in many of their feelings the ancient Egyptians were. Hieroglyphs offer a glimpse into an earlier world and into the customs, hopes, and fears of the people who lived in it long ago. This book has shown just a small part of what there is to learn about ancient Egypt and its writing and will perhaps encourage you to read more.

SOME IMPORTANT KINGS AND
THEIR DYNASTIES

ARCHAIC PERIOD

First Dynasty   (3100–2890 B.C.)
NARMER

Second Dynasty   (2890–2686 B.C.)
RANEB

Third Dynasty   (2686–2613 B.C.)
DJOSER

OLD KINGDOM

Fourth Dynasty   (2613–2494 B.C.)
CHEOPS
CHEPHREN
MYCERINIUS

Fifth Dynasty   (2494–2345 B.C.)
SAHURA
UNAS

Sixth Dynasty   (2345–2181 B.C.)
TETI
PEPY I
PEPY II

First Intermediate Period: Seventh Through Tenth Dynasty (2181–2133 B.C.)

This was a troubled period, in which Egypt was divided into many small kingdoms, each with a different ruler.

MIDDLE KINGDOM

Eleventh Dynasty   (2133–1991 b.c.)

Twelfth Dynasty   (1991–1786 b.c.)
AMENEMHAT I, II and III
SESOSTRIS I, II and III

Thirteenth Dynasty   (1786–1633 b.c.)
SEBEKHOTEP III

Second Intermediate Period (1633–1567 b.c.)
Many kings ruled Egypt in this period, and the country was invaded
by people from Palestine.

NEW KINGDOM

Eighteenth Dynasty   (1567–1320 b.c.)
QUEEN HATSHEPSUT
TUTHMOSIS I, II, III, IV
AMENHOTEP I, II, III
AMENHOTEP IV (AKHENATEN)
QUEEN NEFERTITI
TUTANKHAMEN

Nineteenth Dynasty   (1320–1200 b.c.)
SETY I
RAMESSES II

Twentieth Dynasty   (1200–1085 b.c.)
RAMESSES III

Third Intermediate Period (1085–750 b.c.)
This was again a period of many kings; those in the north were weak;
in the south, priests acted as kings.

LATE PERIOD

Twenty-fifth Dynasty	(Kings from Nubia) (750–656 B.C.) TAHARQO
Twenty-sixth Dynasty	(656–525 B.C.) PSAMTIK II AMASIS
Twenty-seventh Dynasty	(Kings from Persia) (525–404 B.C.) DARIUS I
Thirtieth Dynasty	(404–343 B.C.) NECTANEBO I
Alexander the Great	(343–323 B.C.)
Ptolemaic Period	(323–30 B.C.) PTOLEMY I–XII CLEOPATRA VII

All photographs, unless otherwise stated, courtesy of the Department of Egyptian and Classical Art, the Brooklyn Museum.

Page 6   London, The British Museum.
Page 8   New York, Metropolitan Museum of Art neg. no. MM 61282 B.
Page 11   Brooklyn acc.no. 52.73. Charles Edwin Wilbour Fund.
Page 12   Brooklyn acc.no. 37.440E. Charles Edwin Wilbour Fund.
Page 13   Brooklyn acc.no. 48.27. Charles Edwin Wilbour Fund.
Page 14   New York, Metropolitan Museum of Art acc.no. 01.4.1. Gift of the Egypt Exploration Fund, 1901.
Page 15   Brooklyn acc.no. 50.128. Charles Edwin Wilbour Fund.
Page 17   London, The British Museum.
Page 21   From *Incontro con l'arte egiziana* by Boris de Rachewiltz (Milano, 1958), pl. 3.
Page 22   Brooklyn acc.no. 78.39. Gift of Christ G. Bastis.
Page 23   Bildarchiv Foto Marburg neg.no. 86690.
Page 25   Berkeley, Lowie Museum of Anthropology acc.no. 6–19825.
Page 28   Brooklyn acc.no. 07.420. Museum Collection Fund.
Page 29   New York Metropolitan Museum of Art acc.no. 14.2.7. Rogers Fund, 1914.
Page 30   Brooklyn acc.no. 07.422. Museum Collection Fund.
Page 31   Paris, Archives Photographiques neg.no. MNLE 161 A. © Arch. Phot. Paris.
Page 32   New York Metropolitan Museum of Art acc.no. 12.183.8. Gift of J. Pierpont Morgan, 1912.
Page 34   Boston, Museum of Fine Arts, acc.no. 20.1826.
Page 36   New York Metropolitan Museum of Art. Photograph by Egyptian Expedition.
Page 37   Paris, Archives Photographiques neg.no. E 907. © Arch. Phot. Paris.
Page 40   Berkeley, Lowie Museum of Anthropology acc.no. 6–15174.
Page 41   Chicago, Oriental Institute Museum.
Page 42   Brooklyn acc.no. 35.1998. Charles Edwin Wilbour Fund.
Page 43   London, The British Museum no. 9999.
Page 46   Bildarchiv Foto Marburg neg.no. 216982.

INDEX